Sadie
BRAVES THE
WILDERNESS

YVONNE PEARSON

ILLUSTRATIONS BY KAREN RITZ

MINNESOTA
HISTORICAL
SOCIETY PRESS

For my brave boys, Theo and Archer. —YP

For Jack and Grace and our next adventures. —KR

www.mnhspress.org

The Minnesota Historical Society Press is a member of the Association of American University Presses.

Manufactured in Malaysia

Book design by bedesign, inc.

10 9 8 7 6 5 4 3 2 1

∞ The paper used in this publication meets the minimum requirements of the American National
Standard for Information Sciences—Permanence for Printed Library Materials, ANSI Z39.48-1984.

International Standard Book Number
ISBN: 978-1-68134-038-8 (hardcover)

Library of Congress Cataloging-in-Publication Data available upon request.

We drove for a hundred hours
past a lake called Superior.
It was as big as the ocean.

We drove for a hundred more hours
on a skinny road through a thousand trees,
deeper and deeper into the woods,
until the road turned into dirt and
there were no more houses or people, just us.

"We've arrived at the Boundary Waters," said Dad.
"Hop out."
"Benjamin is very scared of the wilderness," I warned.
"Are you scared, Sadie?" Mom asked.
"No, not me. Benjamin is the one who's scared."

The first day, we climbed a cliff a mile high.
Benjamin was very, very scared.
Monster boulders tried to stop us.
A screeching hawk tried to stop us.
Ripe blueberries stopped me
—but just for a minute.

From the top of the cliff,
we could see the whole world.
I held on to Benjamin
so he wouldn't fall over the edge.

The second day, we swam in a pool
under a waterfall.
Benjamin was really scared,
but I showed him how to be brave.

The waterfall roared and bellowed.
I bellowed back and shook my fists.
Then Benjamin dared to jump in.

The third day, we hiked a dark and twisting forest trail.
At every turn I yelled, "Hey, bear, get out of there."
I sang at the top of my lungs.
When we got to the end, my whole family said,
"Thank goodness we're here."

We launched the canoe on a narrow lake.

Benjamin was still scared, but just a little.

He saw an alligator in front of us.

I shoved it away with a stick.

He saw a flying dinosaur above us.
I blasted it away with my breath.

The last day of our trip,
we were trapped in our tent by a huge storm.
Benjamin was really scared.
He needed me.

The wind whipped branches near the tent.
Benjamin trembled.
I told him, "Don't worry. You are brave."
The trees groaned and creaked.
Benjamin covered his eyes.

I told him, "Don't worry.
The trees are strong."
The rain beat down on the lake.
I grabbed Benjamin's hand.
I told him, "Don't worry.
The lake doesn't mind being wet."

When the storm stopped, I took Benjamin outside
and we played chase through all the new little rivers
until Mom and Dad said, "Time for bed.
We go home early in the morning."

All night I dreamed of next year's trip
to the wild, wild north,
to the wilderness.